MATCHED WITH DANGER

E.B. FOX

CHAPTER ONE

Lilliana

THE SHRILL SOUND of my alarm pierces the air, and I reluctantly open my green eyes to face another day. With a soft groan, I roll out of bed, my long wavy brown hair cascading down my back as I make my way to the bathroom. My reflection in the mirror shows a tired woman with ambition etched into every line of her face. I'm only twenty-nine, but I feel forty some days.

"Time to put on the mask," I whisper to myself, expertly applying makeup to enhance my features. The corporate world has no room for vulnerability, and I've become adept at hiding any sign of it.

"Morning, Lilliana!" Sophie's cheerful voice greets

me as I step into our office. Her vibrant blonde hair bounces with each word, and I can't help but envy her seemingly endless energy.

"Hey, Sophie," I respond, forcing a smile that doesn't quite reach my eyes. "Ready for another day of marketing magic?"

"Always!" she exclaims, her enthusiasm infectious despite my own weariness. We dive into our tasks, and I find myself lost in the familiar rhythm of client meetings, proposals, and reports. Every detail must be perfect; there's no room for error in my work.

As the hours pass, I feel the weight of dissatisfaction grow heavier on my shoulders. It's impressive how a career that once ignited such passion now leaves me feeling empty. Somehow, I crave something more.

"Hey, you okay?" Sophie asks during our lunch break, her perceptive eyes studying me with concern. "You seem...off."

"Can I be honest with you?" I ask hesitantly, unsure if I'm ready to expose my inner turmoil. She nods, her attention solely focused on me.

"I just...I don't know if this is enough anymore, Soph. I feel like I'm drowning in the monotony of it all. There's no spark, no excitement." I sigh, feeling the truth of my words weigh heavily on my chest.

"Maybe you need to explore something new,"

Sophie suggests gently, her hand resting on mine. "You're a passionate woman, Lilliana. You deserve to feel alive."

"Like what?" I question, desperate for answers that seem impossible to find.

"Have you considered exploring your desires? Trying something...kinky?" she asks boldly, her eyes sparkling with a hint of mischief. It's a side of her I've always admired, and part of me wonders if embracing my inner vixen could be the key to unlocking the satisfaction I crave.

"Kinky?" I repeat, allowing the word to roll off my tongue and savor every syllable. "That's...not something I've ever really thought about."

I've honestly not had many boyfriends. I'm no virgin, but, hell, it's been so long I might as well be. And my sex life with the few boyfriends I've had has been pretty lackluster to say the least.

"Maybe it's time you did," Sophie encourages, her voice filled with conviction. "Who knows, maybe it'll unlock an entirely new world for you."

"Maybe," I agree hesitantly, the seed of curiosity now firmly planted within me. As I return to my work, I can't help but wonder if this is the missing piece to my puzzle. Can indulging in my deepest desires truly set me free?

CHAPTER TWO

Lilliana

LYING ON MY SILK SHEETS, I can't shake Sophie's words from earlier tonight. She had such conviction as she told me, "You need to explore your desires, Lilliana. Life's too short not to."

"Fine," I whisper to myself, picking up my phone and downloading the dating app she recommended. I feel a rush of excitement course through my veins as the app opens. Swiping through countless faces, I can't help but think this is the perfect way to push my boundaries.

Then, Dash Harper appears on my screen, and I'm instantly captivated. His jet-black hair frames piercing blue eyes that seem to stare into my very soul. Hesitating for just a moment, I swipe right, and a match notification pops up immediately.

Hey there, Lilliana, the message reads, causing an involuntary shiver to run down my spine.

Hi, Dash, I type back, biting my lip in anticipation.

Our conversation flows with ease, full of innu-endos and suggestive language that leaves me breath-less. His confidence is intoxicating. He talks about what he'd do to me like he knows exactly what I crave.

And it shocks me when he says, *I bet you're looking for a daddy, aren't you?*

I've never thought about calling a man 'daddy' before, but something about the way Dash suggests it sends heat straight to my core.

Maybe, I type back. *I've never had one before.*

Dash gets what I'm saying because he types back, *You've been waiting for the right man. I bet you're such a good girl.*

I bite my lip as I press my thighs together. Why does his praise turn me on so much?

Tell me something naughty you want to try, Dash, I type, feeling my cheeks flush.

Let's save that for when we meet, shall we? he replies, a devilish grin seemingly present in his words.

Dash: *How about dinner tomorrow night? There's an upscale restaurant I've been dying to try.*

Me: *Okay. I'll see you there.*

———

The next night as I anxiously await Dash's arrival, I sit at the dimly lit bar of the upscale restaurant, my heart pounding in my chest. As I sip my wine, the door opens, and I catch a glimpse of him entering the room.

He's tall and broad-shouldered, with a chiseled jawline and intense blue eyes. His presence fills the room like an electric current, and I feel myself drawn to him. As he strides closer, his cologne hangs in the air, and my heart beats faster.

"Hello, Lilliana," he murmurs, his voice sending shivers down my spine. "You look stunning."

"Thank you," I reply softly, unable to tear my eyes away from his. The connection is electrifying. It's as if our desires are already intertwined.

"Let's get a table," he suggests, and I nod, feeling a mixture of excitement and vulnerability.

As we sit down, Dash leans in closer, his breath hot on my ear as he whispers, "I can't wait to have you begging for my touch, calling me daddy."

My heart races at the thought, and I struggle to maintain my composure while the waiter takes our order. The entire meal is filled with suggestive comments and stolen touches that make it nearly impossible to focus on anything else.

"Ready to find out what I have planned for tonight?" Dash asks, his voice low and seductive.

"Absolutely," I respond, my voice barely audible.

"Good girl," he praises, sending a thrill through my body. We leave the restaurant, anticipation building with every step as we embark on this journey of exploration and desire together.

CHAPTER THREE

Lilliana

"COME ON, I have a surprise for you," Dash says with a smoldering look as he takes my hand, leading me away from the bustling restaurant.

My heart races in anticipation, my eyes wide with excitement. As we reach a hidden door down a dimly lit alley, Dash gently pushes me against the wall, his piercing blue eyes locking onto mine.

"Are you ready to experience something truly thrilling, Lilliana?" he whispers, his breath hot against my ear.

"God, yes," I respond, my voice shaking with desire. I trust Dash completely—which is surprisingly considering that I'm not some doe-eyed, naïve little girl

—and the thought of him introducing me to something new only heightens my yearning.

He smirks, opening the secret door and guiding me into the speakeasy. The room is filled with sultry jazz music, couples swaying to the beat in intimate embrace. The atmosphere is thick with passion, and I feel myself becoming intoxicated by the scent of lust that lingers in the air.

"Let's dance," Dash suggests, pulling me close to him as we join the other couples on the dance floor.

Our bodies meld together, moving rhythmically as one. I can feel the heat radiating off of Dash's body, making me ache to be even closer to him. As he twirls me around, our gazes lock, and I can see the hunger in his eyes.

"Tell me, baby girl," he growls in my ear, "do you want me to take control tonight? To show you just how good it can feel to let someone else call the shots?"

"Y-yes," I stammer, my mind racing with erotic images of being dominated by this powerful man. I realize then that Dash could be the excitement I've been craving in my life, the intoxicating rush of adrenaline I've been searching for in every controlled corner of my existence.

There's an air of danger about him. It's something that should probably concern me, but it doesn't.

Instead, it draws me in like a moth to a flame.

"Good," he purrs, pressing his lips against my neck and sending shivers down my spine. "I want to hear you beg for it, Lilliana. I want you to say, 'Please, Daddy, let me be your good girl.'"

"Please, Daddy," I whisper, feeling a thrill course through me as the words pass my lips, "let me be your good girl."

"God, you're so fucking sexy when you talk like that," Dash groans, pulling me even closer against him. Our dance becomes more and more heated, our bodies grinding together as our lust threatens to consume us.

Our bodies move in sync, swaying to the sultry jazz music that fills the air. The atmosphere is electric, and Dash and I can't seem to keep our hands off of each other. His hands grip my waist tightly as we move together, sending sparks of pleasure radiating through me.

I can feel the heat radiating from his body, and it only serves to fuel my desire. His lips brush against my neck, sending shivers down my spine, and I feel myself melting into him.

We become lost in our own little world—there's no one else around us—just Dash and I getting lost in each other's arms. His hands wander all over me, exploring every curve of my body with gentle caresses.

My heart pounds, and I feel an overwhelming sensation of pleasure coursing through me.

Dash pulls away suddenly, locking his intense gaze on mine. "Let's get out of here," he whispers gruffly, taking my hand in his own and leading me away from the speakeasy and into a hidden back alleyway.

The darkness envelops us as Dash pushes me up against the wall of the alleyway, pressing his body against mine. He takes my face in his hands and captures my lips in a passionate kiss that leaves me breathless. His tongue explores every inch of my mouth as our bodies writhe together in pleasure.

His kiss is intoxicating—it's like a drug that leaves me wanting more—*needing* more—and soon I'm begging for him to take control as I surrender completely to his touch.

"Let's me take you home," he suggests, his voice ragged with need. "I have so much more I want to show you tonight, baby girl."

"Take me there, Daddy" I reply, ready to embrace this new side of myself, to submit to the exhilarating passion Dash has awakened within me.

CHAPTER FOUR

Lilliana

THE SOUND of Dash's keys jingling as he unlocks the door to his apartment sends a shiver down my spine. The anticipation has been building all night, and now we're finally here. He opens the door and ushers me in, his strong hand on the small of my back guiding me forward.

"Home sweet home," he says, his voice low and husky as he closes the door behind him.

"Nice place," I reply, trying to sound nonchalant but feeling my heart pound in my chest. It's a spacious loft with exposed brick walls, an open floor plan, and modern furnishings. Dash has an aura of power about him anyway, but now it's crystal clear just what kind of wealth this man has. It's honestly a bit intimidating.

Dash steps closer to me, and without a word, he pulls me into his embrace. Our lips meet in a passionate kiss, and it's as if a fire ignites within me. All my reservations melt away as his tongue explores my mouth, sending waves of desire coursing through my body. My hands find their way to his hair, tugging at the dark locks as our kiss deepens.

"God, I've wanted this since the moment I laid eyes on you," he whispers against my lips. "You have no idea what you do to me, Lilliana."

"Show me," I breathe out, my voice barely audible.

Dash wastes no time complying. He leads me toward the bedroom, where a massive king-sized bed awaits, draped in luxurious black silk sheets. He pushes me down onto the bed and crawls on top of me, his piercing blue eyes never leaving mine.

"Tell me what you want," he demands, his voice low and seductive.

"I...I want you," I stammer, my cheeks flushing red from embarrassment.

"Be more specific, baby girl," he teases, grinding his hips against mine. "What do you want me to do to you?"

"Fuck me, Dash," I beg, my voice coming out as a throaty whisper. "Please fuck me."

His eyes darken with lust at my words, and he begins to strip off our clothes with an urgency that matches my own. Soon, we're both naked, our bodies pressed together, the heat between us almost unbearable.

"Tell me if it's too much, Lilliana," he warns, his fingers teasing my entrance. "I don't want to hurt you."

"Dash, please," I whimper, unable to contain my desire any longer. "I need you inside me."

"Such a needy little thing, aren't you?" he chuckles, but his voice holds nothing but desire. "Alright, baby girl, you asked for it."

Without further ado, he pushes into me, filling me completely. I gasp at the sensation, feeling both pain and pleasure intermingling within me. Fuck, he's bigger than any man I've ever been with, and I'm starting to wonder if this was a good idea. But as he starts to move, the pleasure quickly overtakes the pain, and I can't help but cry out in ecstasy.

"God, Lilliana, you feel so fucking good," Dash growls, his breath hot against my ear. "Tight as a fucking virgin, aren't you? You been a good girl, saving yourself for your daddy, haven't you? You were made for me, weren't you?"

"Yes, Daddy," I moan, thrilling at the possessiveness in his words. "Only for you."

As our bodies move together, it feels like we're in perfect sync. The intensity of our lovemaking increases with every thrust, every touch, and every shared moan. It's as if all the pent-up emotions from our pasts have been unleashed, allowing us to connect on a level neither of us has ever experienced before.

"That's it," Dash huffs in my ear. "Feel how I fill you like none of those other fuckers ever could? You're mine now, Lilliana. All *mine*. Going to make sure the only cock you ever want inside you again is mine."

My pussy clenches at his possessive words. I don't know what I like them so much, but I do.

"Oh fuck yeah," Dash groans as he feels me fluttering around him. "Are you close, baby girl?" he asks, his voice strained with effort.

"Y-yes, Daddy," I stammer, my body trembling with the impending orgasm.

"Come for me, Lilliana," he commands, his own release imminent. "Come for your daddy."

With those words, I shatter into a million pieces, my climax crashing over me like a tidal wave. Dash follows suit, his own orgasm wracking his body as he spills himself deep inside me.

"Dash," I whisper, tears prickling at the corners of

my eyes. The closeness we've shared tonight has opened up a vulnerability in both of us that's impossible to ignore.

"Shh, Lilliana," he murmurs, pulling me close against his chest. "We'll figure everything out tomorrow. For now, let's just enjoy this moment together."

And so, wrapped in each other's arms, we drift off to sleep, our bodies and souls entwined as one.

CHAPTER FIVE

Dash

THE MORNING SUNLIGHT streams through the curtains, casting a warm glow on Lilliana's sleeping form beside me. Her wavy brown hair cascades over the pillow like a waterfall, and her soft breaths send shivers down my spine. I can't help but think about how she made me feel last night.

"Dash, please," she begged, her green eyes wide with desire, "I need you inside me."

My hands roam over her supple skin as I remember the way she arched her back and moaned my name when I finally granted her wish. The taste of her lips still lingers on mine, sweet and intoxicating. My body aches with the memory of our passionate union, the way we fit together so perfectly. The sound of her voice whispering sinful promises in my ear sends a jolt of electricity through me.

"Fuck me harder, Daddy," she panted, her nails digging into my shoulders as I pounded into her relentlessly.

I've never wanted anyone as much as I want Lilliana, and it scares me. I know I'd do anything to have her, to keep her by my side.

But there's a darkness within me that she doesn't know about yet. My criminal past—and present—the risks I've taken, and the things I've done.

She's so pure and innocent, a bright light in the shadows of my existence. And yet, I'm selfish enough to taint her for my own desires. A pang of guilt washes over me, but the thought of losing her is unbearable.

"Dash?" Lilliana's sleepy voice pulls me from my thoughts as she stirs beside me. "What are you thinking about?"

"Last night," I admit, my voice rough with emotion. "It was...incredible, Lilliana."

Her cheeks flush a deep pink, and her eyes sparkle with happiness. "It was, wasn't it? I've never felt anything like that before."

"Neither have I," I confess, the weight of my secrets pressing down on me.

But I can't tell her.

Not yet.

And as I look into her beautiful, trusting gaze, I make a silent vow to protect her at all costs—even if it means losing myself in the process.

CHAPTER SIX

Lilliana

"REMEMBER that guy I met online? Dash?" I ask, sitting on the edge of my bed with Sophie sprawled across its surface. My heart races at the thought of him, my body tingling with excitement.

"Ooh, Mr. Tall, Dark and Handsome," Sophie teases, grinning widely. "What happened? Do tell!"

"Last night, we went on a date, and it was...incredible," I confess, my voice barely above a whisper. As I look into Sophie's eager eyes, I can't help but feel a wave of embarrassment wash over me. She's always been more adventurous than I am, but now, for the first time in my life, I feel alive, daring, and utterly consumed by desire.

"Give me all the juicy details!" she demands, her blue eyes sparkling with anticipation.

"Okay, so we started off at this cozy little restaurant in the city," I say, pausing to gather my thoughts. "The conversation was amazing. He's so...different, Sophie. He has this air of mystery about him that I just can't resist."

"Sounds like you've got it bad," Sophie giggles as she wiggles her eyebrows suggestively. "So, what happened next?"

"Dash took me to his apartment, and that's when things got...intense." The memory sends shivers down my spine, and I bite my lip, recalling the way he made me feel. "We ended up in his bedroom, and, well, let's just say he introduced me to a whole new world of pleasure."

"Wow, Lilliana! I never expected you'd be into something like that!" Sophie exclaims, clearly surprised. "But hey, good for you! So, what exactly did you guys do?"

I hesitate for a moment, wondering if I should really share the intimate details of my experience with Dash. But Sophie is my best friend, and I trust her implicitly.

"Dash...he called me his dirty little girl," I admit, feeling my cheeks grow hot at the admission. "And I...I loved it."

"Ooh, so you've got a daddy kink, huh?" Sophie says with a sly smile, not an ounce of judgment in her voice. "That's pretty hot, Lil. How does Dash make you feel?"

"Alive, Sophie," I confess, my heart pounding in my chest. "With him, all my inhibitions just seem to melt away. It's like I'm discovering a whole new side of myself that I never knew existed."

"Embrace it, Lilliana," she encourages, her eyes full of love and support. "You deserve to be happy and explore your desires. Just remember to stay safe and communicate openly with Dash."

"Thanks, Sophie," I say, feeling grateful for her understanding and acceptance. "I still can't believe this is happening, but I can't wait to see where this journey takes me."

"Neither can I," Sophie replies, grinning from ear to ear. "Now, let's go celebrate your newfound sexual awakening!"

CHAPTER SEVEN

Lilliana

"COME ON, LILLIANA, LET'S CELEBRATE!"
Sophie exclaims, grabbing my arm as we walk into the
dimly lit club. The bass from the music pulsates
through my body, awakening my senses. My heart
races with anticipation, my cautious nature momentarily set aside for a night of excitement.

I laugh and allow her infectious energy to take
over. As we make our way to the dance floor, I can't
help but feel alive and free.

I'm soon lost in the rhythm of the music, my body
swaying seductively along with the beat. A stranger

approaches me, his hands finding their way to my hips as he dances close to me. Normally, I would be hesitant, but tonight is different. Tonight, I allow myself to be swept up in the moment.

"Having fun, aren't you?" the stranger whispers into my ear, his warm breath sending shivers down my spine. I nod, biting my lip, as I grind against him, feeling a thrill that I've longed for.

Just then, Dash appears out of nowhere. His piercing blue eyes are filled with rage as he takes in the scene before him. Without warning, he delivers a powerful punch to the stranger's face, knocking him out cold.

"Dash, what the hell?!" I exclaim, shocked by his sudden appearance and violent reaction.

"Nobody touches what's mine," he growls, grabbing my arm and pulling me toward the exit. I stumble, struggling to keep up with his forceful pace. My thoughts race. I should be pissed, terrified, but there's a part of me that craves this possessiveness, this dark side of Dash.

Once we're at his apartment, Dash doesn't waste any time. He pushes me against the wall, pinning me with his strong arms. "You're mine, Lilliana. You understand that?" he demands, his eyes burning into mine.

"Y-yes," I stutter, my heart pounding in my chest. Dash kisses me roughly, his tongue dominating mine. He tears off my clothes, leaving me exposed and vulnerable under his intense gaze.

"Get on the bed," he orders, and I obey without question. He follows, stripping off his own clothes to reveal his muscular body. "I'm going to remind you who you belong to."

His fingers dig into my hips as he thrusts into me, hard and fast. Every inch of my body screams in pleasure and pain, but I can't deny how much I crave this roughness from him. The way he dominates me, possesses me—it's everything I've secretly desired.

"Fuck, Lilliana... You're so tight," he groans, his voice thick with lust. "You like it when I fuck you like this, don't you? When I remind you who your daddy is?"

"Y-yes, Daddy," I moan, overwhelmed by the intensity of the moment. My mind races with the taboo nature of our exchange, yet I can't help but feel a sense of belonging, of being owned by Dash.

"Good girl," he praises, his thrusts becoming more erratic. As he reaches his climax, he leans down, his breath hot against my ear. "If I ever see another man touch you again, I'll fucking kill him. You understand?"

"Y-yes, Dash," I reply, my voice shaking. I know

he's not kidding. The manic look in his eyes tells me that he's deadly serious. A chill runs down my spine, but deep down, there's a part of me that finds comfort in his possessiveness, in knowing that I am *his* and his alone.

CHAPTER EIGHT

Lilliana

THE SCENT of Dash's cologne lingers in the air, wrapping around me like a warm embrace. Our bodies are tangled together on the bed, skin still flushed from our passionate love-making. I nuzzle my face into his chest. Despite how he went all caveman on me, I'd be lying if I didn't admit that I loved it.

"You're mine, baby girl," Dash murmurs, his fingers tracing lazy patterns on my bare back. The way he calls me "baby girl" sends a shiver down my spine. It's equal parts comforting and erotic, and I crave more of him—more of this delicious intimacy we share.

"Tell me something about yourself, Daddy," I say, propping myself up on one elbow to look into his piercing blue eyes. He hesitates for a moment, his brow furrowing in thought. This isn't the first time Dash has been evasive when it comes to his past, and my curiosity piques.

Just when I think he's not going to answer, he speaks slowly. "Before I got into my current line of work, I used to be a race car driver." As he speaks, I can't help but notice the tension in his body. My instincts tell me there's more to the story, but I don't want to push him too far.

"Wow, that's exciting!" I respond, trying to keep the conversation light. "What made you quit?"

"Let's just say I had my reasons," he replies, a shadow crossing his face. My mind races with possibilities, and my previous suspicions only grow stronger. What is he hiding from me? I need to find out, but I won't get any answers tonight when he pulls me closer and crashes his lips onto mine. We lose ourselves in each other once more, but as our bodies move together in perfect harmony, I can't shake the feeling that there's a part of Dash I have yet to discover.

In the days that follow, I become increasingly determined to unravel the mystery of Dash Harper. It starts with innocent Google searches and social media stalking, but soon escalates to digging through public records and reaching out to people who might have known him before he entered my life.

As I delve deeper into his past, I find myself more and more intrigued—and not just by the secrets he keeps. I'm drawn to the darkness within him, and I crave the thrill of exploring his kinks and desires. At times, it feels like I'm leading a double life: the perfect marketing executive by day, and Dash's devoted submissive by night.

Yet, despite the undeniable connection between us, I know there's still a piece of the puzzle missing. And as I continue my investigation, I can't help but worry about what I might uncover. Will finding the truth bring us even closer? Or will it shatter the fragile bond we've built?

Only time will tell, but one thing is certain: I won't rest until I know everything there is to know about Dash Harper, the man who has awakened something within me that I never knew existed.

CHAPTER NINE

Lilliana

THE OPULENT CHANDELIER above casts a golden glow on the partygoers as Dash leads me through the grand entrance of Lucas King's mansion. My heart beats a staccato rhythm in my chest when we enter the extravagant space.

Everyone knows who Lucas King is, and the fact that Dash is acquainted enough with the criminal under lord to be invited to one of his parties is only affirmation about my suspicions about Dash's dark side.

As dangerous as I know this scene is, the hum of

conversation around us, mixed with the clinking of champagne flutes, creates an intoxicating symphony of indulgence. I can't help but be captivated.

"Enjoying yourself, princess?" Dash whispers into my ear, his warm breath sending shivers down my spine.

"Very much so," I reply, my eyes darting around the room to take in the lavish decorations and well-dressed guests. "I've never been to a party like this before."

"Lucas only throws the best," he says with a sly grin, pulling me closer by my waist. "Just remember to stick close to me. There are some dangerous people here."

As if on cue, a Spanish beauty enters my line of sight. Her dark hair is pulled back into a tight bun, and her sharp brown eyes seem to miss nothing as they survey the room. She carries herself with a confidence that both intrigues and frightens me. I can tell she's not someone to cross paths with.

"Who's that woman?" I ask, unable to tear my gaze away from her.

"Rosa Martinez," Dash answers, his voice low and cautious. "One of Lucas' most trusted associates. She's cunning and ruthless, so keep your distance."

"Understood," I say, swallowing hard as I watch

Rosa engage in conversation with a group of men who exude an air of danger.

Throughout the night, I find myself drawn to the extravagant lifestyle on display. The way the silk fabric of my dress brushes against my skin makes me feel undeniably desirable, and the seductive glances Dash shoots me only heighten that feeling. But even as I sip expensive champagne and engage in flirtatious banter with other guests, the uneasiness I feel around the criminal figures in the room never quite dissipates.

"Dash," I murmur, pulling him aside and lowering my voice to a sultry whisper, "I need you. *Now.*"

"Right here?" he teases, his blue eyes darkening. "In front of all these people? A new kink you'd like to explore, baby girl?"

"Of course not," I say, my cheeks heating at the image he's painting. "Find us somewhere private."

"Your wish is my command, princess," Dash replies, taking my hand and leading me down a dimly lit hallway, away from the festivities.

As soon as we're alone, I fling my arms around Dash and kiss him desperately. Dash must sense the turmoil roiling within me because he grabs my arms and looks down at me.

He stares at me for a long moment before his mouth firms into a grim line. "I want you to know,

Lilliana, you have nothing to worry about when you're with me. I'll always protect you."

I don't say anything. Instead, I kiss him again, wanting to feel the connection that we achieve with our bodies.

Dash deepens the kiss, his possessiveness anchoring me like a lifeline.

I climb up into his arms like a monkey, wrapping my legs around him and humping against his hardness through our clothes, desperate for him to make me come.

"I need you, Dash," I say, surprised by the desperation in my own voice. "I *need* to feel your cock in me."

Dash laughs into my mouth. "My good girl needs her daddy, doesn't she?"

I fucking love that he can feel me coming undone. I love it even more when he pins me against the wall and rips off my panties. I push my hips out and Dash gives me exactly what I want, plunging his cock all the way to the hilt in one hard thrust.

"Yes, Daddy," I manage to gasp out, rocking my hips against his. Dash grips me tightly by the hips and fucks me hard, his length stretching me open.

I'm so close to coming, but I know if I'm going to do it, I need more friction. "Fuck me from behind," I say, barely breathing as I grind against him.

I feel Dash's cock twitch inside me at my words, and he pulls out just as I push myself up and turn around. I place my hands on the wall and arch my back, my ass sticking out. I hear Dash's sharp intake of breath as his gaze travels down my body. He rakes his eyes over me, then back up before he fists his cock and smacks my ass with it.

"You've been a bad girl, Lilliana," he says, and I can hear the lust in his voice.

"You'll have to punish me later, Daddy."

"Spank you until your ass is red and you can't sit down?"

"Please, Daddy."

Dash groans and graze his cock up and down my pussy before lining it up with my entrance. I feel his hands on my hips, his fingers gripping my flesh as he presses slowly, slowly into me. His other hand comes around to find my clit and he drags his thumb across it, making me cry out and arch my back, pushing my ass back further in invitation.

Dash sighs at the movement and grips my hips harder, driving his cock into me with renewed urgency. His thumb is still on my clit, rubbing back and forth, making me moan and grind back against him.

Dash pulls out of me and I feel his hand on my

shoulder, turning me around. I want to protest, feeling the loss of his cock, but then his mouth is on me, licking my breasts, before he uses his teeth to pull one of my nipples into his mouth.

I moan as he sucks, the sensation so intense I can barely stand it. He smiles at my reaction and I feel his cock nudging my entrance again. "Beg for it," he says, his voice a low rasp in my ear.

"Please, Dash, please fuck me."

Dash slams his cock into me, deep and hard, and I moan and push back against him. His thumb is still on my clit, rubbing back and forth, his other hand on my hip, and I feel my orgasm building up in the pit of my stomach once again. Dash leans back and I feel his warm breath on my neck.

Dash bites down on my shoulder hard, and I feel my orgasm overtake me. Wave after wave of pleasure breaks over me, my vision goes white, and I swear I can feel my toes curl.

"You like that, Lilliana?" Dash growls in my ear, his fingers digging into my hips.

"Yes, Daddy," I pant. "Fuck me harder."

Dash slams into me, his other hand coming up to pull my hair. I yelp in pain, but it only makes me wetter.

Dash pulls my hair harder, tugging on it as he

fucks me, his pace getting faster and faster. I can hear his grunts and mine as the pleasure and pain mix and mingle in our ears. For a moment, the world goes away, and all there is is this: the sounds we make, the feeling of his hands and his cock, the way he is making me feel so good.

Dash slows down his pace, pulling out of me and spinning me around so I'm facing the wall. He pushes my legs apart with his knee and I feel him following, positioning himself behind me. I bite my lip and press my forehead against the wall, waiting for him to fuck me again.

But then he changes his mind before he spins me around.

"No," Dash says, his voice stern. "I want you on your knees. Now."

"Yes, Daddy," I say, a thrill running through me at the dominance in his voice.

I feel his hands on my back, urging me to move, and I slowly lower myself to my knees. I look down, his cock hard and waiting for me, and I open my mouth.

Dash grabs my hair, pulling it back as he fucks my face. I look down, staring at his muscled thighs, at the way he fills my mouth.

"Take it," Dash snarls, and his hand tightens on my hair. "Take it all."

His cock slides further into my throat. I can't breathe, and the only thing I can think about is how good it feels to have him there. I try to relax my throat, to let it open up more, and Dash lets go of my hair. I start bobbing my head back and forth, matching his pace, my hands on his thighs.

Dash lets go of his cock with one hand, wrapping it around my throat instead. The feeling of his hand around my throat, of his cock in my mouth, is intoxicating. I feel my pussy throbbing, my juices dripping down my thighs, but I don't think I will come again. I think I am high on this, on the way he is treating me.

Dash slides his cock out of my mouth and pulls me back so that I'm kneeling in front of him, my face in between his legs. He grabs my arms and forces them over my head, pinning me to the floor. I look up at him, our faces close together, and I don't see the calm, in-control Dash that I met just a few weeks ago.

"Do you like this?" Dash rasps, his cock throbbing in front of me. "Do you like being this way?"

I feel my pulse beating in my throat, and I nod.

"Yes, Daddy," I breathe.

"Yes, I know," Dash whispers, leaning in. He puts his hand on my neck and kisses me hard, his tongue forcing its way into my mouth.

I kiss him back, my arms still over my head. I can

feel his cock pressing against my stomach, and I want to reach down and grab it, to stroke it until he comes all over me. But I can't.

"I know you want to come," Dash growls in between kisses. "But you're going to have to wait until I say you can."

"Yes, Daddy," I whisper, kissing him back.

Dash slides his hand under my chin, tilting my face up. He kisses me again, and then he pulls back.

"Good girl," he breathes, looking down at me. He slides his hand down my neck and over my chest, resting it over my heart. "You're going to make me come."

I feel my heart pounding, beating faster under his hand. I look up at him, my eyes wide.

"You're going to make me come," Dash says again. "On your knees and on your stomach."

I nod.

"Get on your knees," Dash growls. He lets go of me and stands up.

I kneel in front of him, my face up against the sofa cushions. Dash pets my hair, then he grabs my waist and pulls me so that my face and upper body is on the floor, while my ass is still in the air. I kneel like this for a few seconds, and then I feel Dash's hand on my lower back.

"Remember how you made me come the other night?" Dash says. "You're going to do that again."

I squeeze my eyes shut, my cheeks flushing.

"Yes, Daddy," I say quietly.

He squeezes my ass hard, pulling it toward him. I open my eyes and look at him over my shoulder. His eyes are dark with lust.

"I'm going to come on your ass," he says. "And in your mouth, and on your face."

I swallow hard. I feel my heart pounding in my chest, a flush spreading over my body. The thought of him coming on me is so hot.

I watch as Dash slides his hand from my lower back down between my legs. I spread my thighs apart for him, and he leans forward, kissing me softly.

"How do you want me to make you come?" he whispers into my ear.

I swallow.

"Come inside me," I breathe.

I grab his cock and guide it to my pussy. Dash slides it into me slowly, and I feel myself closing around him, gripping him tightly.

Dash leans forward and kisses me as he starts fucking me. My nipples brush against the cushions of the sofa, and I moan into his mouth as he starts to fuck me harder, sliding his cock into me deeper and harder.

Dash rolls his hips and pulls his cock almost all the way out of me, then he slams it back in.

I dig my nails into his back as he fucks me. I'm so wet that we're both panting. Dash groans, and he kisses me harder. I moan into his mouth as I feel his cock twitch inside me.

I feel Dash's body tensing against me. He pulls out of me, and without warning, he slides his cock into my ass. I tilt my face up, moaning loudly. His cock slides into my ass and I exhale sharply as I feel his body on top of me. Dash kisses me again, and I wrap my arms around him, pulling him close.

Dash fucks my ass slowly, and I feel my pussy getting wetter. He grabs my lower back and pulls me up against him, so that he's supporting me against his chest. I moan softly into his mouth as he fucks me.

"Yes," I breathe softly, my breath warm against his lips.

Dash closes his eyes and kisses me again. His body is pressed against mine, and he's fucking me so hard that I have to hold on to him.

"I'm going to come in your ass," he whispers.

I can feel myself getting closer to coming. I squeeze my eyes shut and kiss him softly as I feel him thrusting into me faster

and faster.

"Please come in my ass," I moan. "Please."

"Say it again," Dash says, his voice deep.

I look up at Dash, and I look deep into his eyes.

"Please come in my ass," I moan, and my voice catches as Dash pushes his cock into me even deeper.

"Fuck, baby," he whispers, our faces so close that our lips are almost touching. "Oh my God, I'm going to come."

I tip my head back as I feel Dash's cock twitching deep in my ass. He grabs my shoulders and pulls me against him, so he's thrusting into me even harder, and I feel my pussy starting to clench.

Dash groans.

"Oh fuck, Lilliana!"

Dash has both his hands on my shoulders, and he's fucking me hard and deep. I can feel his cock twitching inside me. He holds my shoulders tight and moans.

"Oh, fuck. Oh, my God, Lilliana. Oh, fucking fuck."

Dash's body is shaking as he comes inside my ass. I can feel his cock jerking and his body twitching against me.

"Oh, God, Dash," I moan, as I feel his hot cum shooting into me.

I feel my pussy clenching, and I come hard. Dash

smashes his lips onto mine, and I moan into his mouth as I come.

Dash's cock is twitching and jerking deep in my ass, and I can feel his warm cum dripping out of my ass and down over my pussy.

And then he rolls me over and proceeds to do everything he promised.

And I allow myself to get lost in the passion and excitement of the night, focusing on Dash's strong hands guiding me and the exhilarating feeling of danger mixed with desire.

CHAPTER TEN

Dash

"WHERE IS SHE?" I snarl into my phone, pacing my living room like a caged animal. I hadn't anticipated Lilliana running away from me after our passionate encounter at the party. I dropped her safely off at home—against my better judgment. Every instinct in me had screamed for me to take her home with me, but when she wanted to go to her place, I tried to respect her wishes.

Now, all I can think about is the thought of another man's hands on her.

It drives me insane with jealousy.

"Still no sign of her," my informant says cautiously. "But we're still looking."

"Find her," I order, my voice cold with determination. "She will be mine, whether she wants it or not."

Lilliana

My heart pounds in my chest as I glance nervously around the dimly lit parking garage. Dash's threats echo in my mind, making me shiver with fear. Why did I ever let myself get involved with someone so dangerous?

"Going somewhere, princess?" Dash's voice sends a shiver down my spine. I spin around to find him leaning against my car, his piercing blue eyes locked on mine.

"Dash, please," I beg, my voice shaking with desperation. "Let me go."

"Can't do that, sweetheart," he says smoothly, closing the distance between us. "You're all I care about. And if I have to keep you against your will, then so be it." His strong arms wrap around me, pinning me against the cold metal of my car.

"Please," I whisper again, tears streaming down my cheeks. But in the depths of my mind, there's a small part of me that craves his dominance.

"Shh," he murmurs, gently wiping away my tears. "You'll learn to love it, I promise." As he lifts me into his arms and carries me away from the life I once knew, I can't help but wonder if he's right.

CHAPTER ELEVEN

Lilliana

DESPITE THE UNEASE gnawing at my core, I find myself drawn to Dash, unable to resist the magnetic pull of his presence. The dimly lit room casts a seductive glow as we sit on the plush couch of his apartment, our thighs brushing against each other. My heart races with anticipation, fueled by the intoxicating mix of desire and fear.

"Dash," I whisper, my voice wavering slightly, "If you ever want me to trust you, you need to tell me about your connection to Lucas King—and your past."

His piercing blue eyes narrow, and he exhales a

long breath. I can see the internal struggle taking place behind those mysterious eyes. But it's time for me to confront my fears, and I won't back down now.

"Alright, Lilliana," he murmurs, his voice a gravelly mix of reluctance and resignation. "It's true that I was once involved with Lucas and his criminal empire. "But that's behind me now," he goes earnestly. "I've changed."

As he speaks, I notice the tension in his jaw, the way his fingers tap nervously on his thigh. It's clear that this is difficult for him, but I appreciate his honesty. My chest tightens with emotion, and I feel an overwhelming desire to reach out and touch him, to show him that I understand.

"Dash," I say softly, placing my hand on his arm, "I believe you."

His jaw clenches as he turns accusing eyes to me. "You ran from me."

"I'm sorry," I tell him genuinely.

He looks at me, his eyes searching mine, and I see something shift within him. As if a weight has been lifted, his lips relax. Our faces draw closer, and I can feel his warm breath on my skin, sending shivers down my spine.

"If you only knew the depth of my obsession with

you, Lilliana," he murmurs, his voice husky and filled with raw emotion. "You don't know how I need you."

As our lips meet in a tender, passionate kiss, I feel my reservations melt away. I want to explore the depths of this man, to push past our boundaries and uncover the connection that's growing ever stronger between us.

"Dash," I gasp, pulling away from his lips for a moment, "I want you. Take me, show me how much you've changed."

His eyes darken with lust, and he kisses me deeply, his tongue teasing mine as his hand slides up my thigh, fingertips brushing against the sensitive skin beneath my skirt. My body shudders with need, craving the pleasure he promises to unleash.

"I'm going to fuck you hard, Lilliana," he warns, his voice a low growl that sends a jolt of anticipation through my core. "I'm going to push you to your limits today."

"Yes, Daddy," I breathe, surrendering myself completely to the whirlwind of passion and desire that awaits.

My heart races as Dash's piercing blue eyes lock onto mine, his gaze filled with an intensity that sends shivers down my spine. He stands before me, tall and commanding, his sculpted body sending waves of desire through me. Despite my usual cautious nature, I can't help but yearn for the excitement and passion he offers.

"Are you ready, Lilliana?" Dash asks, his voice deep and husky.

I nod, unable to find my voice. His possessive touch as he caresses my cheek sends a thrill through me. I belong to him in this moment, and it feels exhilarating.

"Good girl," he praises, and I feel a surge of pride mingled with lust.

Dash leads me to the bed, every movement exuding confidence and control. Once we reach the edge, he turns to me with a wicked grin and pulls out a gleaming knife from the drawer beside the bed.

"Remember, trust is key," he reminds me, his eyes never leaving mine.

I swallow hard, feeling both fear and anticipation course through my veins. "I trust you, Dash."

"Good," he says, his approval stoking the fire burning within me.

He orders me to undress, and I comply without hesitation. As I stand before him, naked and vulnerable, Dash appraises me with a predatory look that makes my knees weak. The blade glides across my skin, teasing and taunting, leaving goosebumps in its wake. My breath hitches as the cool metal touches my most sensitive spots, threatening to push me over the edge.

"Please," I gasp, my voice a mix of desperation and desire.

"Patience, Lilliana" Dash chastises, his tone firm yet gentle. "I want you to beg for it."

"Dash, please," I whimper, my body quivering with need. "I need you."

"Good girl," he praises again, and I can't help but preen under his words. He places the knife back into the drawer, the absence of its cold touch leaving me feeling bereft.

"Turn around and bend over the bed," Dash commands, and I obey without question. The vulnerability of my position only serves to heighten the anticipation coursing through me.

Suddenly, I feel the sharp sting of his palm connecting with my bare flesh. The pain is quickly replaced by a delicious warmth that spreads across my skin, making me moan in pleasure. A second spank follows, then a third, each one sending shockwaves of pleasure-pain through my body.

"Dash," I gasp, overwhelmed by the sensations flooding me.

"Such a good girl for me, Lilliana," he growls, his

voice tinged with an edge of possessiveness that drives me wild.

With a rough hand, Dash grabs my hair and pulls me up to face him, his blue eyes blazing with desire. "Tell me who you belong to," he demands, his voice thick with lust.

"I belong to you, Dash," I cry out, longing for him to claim me completely.

"Good girl," he murmurs once more, and with a swift motion, he enters me, filling me completely. As he pushes me to my limits, our bodies move together in a dance of passion, dominance, and submission. Together, we find release in a culmination of trust, desire, and love, binding us even closer than before.

CHAPTER TWELVE

Lilliana

"SURPRISE, BABY GIRL," Dash murmurs as I blink my eyes slowly awake.

"Wh-what? Where are we?" I ask as I struggle to sit up.

"Careful," he warns me.

I grip my head as everything spins when I sit up. "Did you fucking drug me?" I ask him admist the pounding in my skull.

He doesn't answer, which is an answer in and of itself.

"Look at where we are, princess," he says instead.

I want to be mad, but my eyes widen as I take in every detail of our luxurious surroundings. We're on a beach, and it's entirely secluded. The luxurious mansion behind us is perfection. As a marketing executive, I'm accustomed to perfection and high standards, but this hideaway exceeds even my expectations.

Still, I can't let him off that easy, so I just glare at him. "Why did you drug me? You had no need to, you fucking psychopath."

"I didn't want to give you the chance to say no."

I bat his hand away when he reaches for me. I grab the water bottle he holds out and take a chug, my mouth dry as cotton.

"Only the best for my beautiful Lilliana," Dash murmurs, his piercing blue eyes locked on mine, making me feel like I'm the only woman in the world. His risk-taking nature is evident in his choice of location, far from prying eyes and what society deems acceptable.

I don't know how long he's had me lying on this bed in the sand sitting over me like a creeper, but he finally helps me stand and we walk toward the mansion.

As soon as we step through the door, I can feel the

electricity between us intensify. In a flash, Dash has shed all our clothing.

"Tell me what you want, baby girl," Dash whispers desperately in my ear, sending a shiver down my spine.

"Please, Daddy, I want you to taste every inch of me and don't stop until I'm begging for mercy," I implore, succumbing to the desires that have been smoldering within me since we met.

"Your wish is my command," Dash responds, his voice full of authority as he gently pushes me back onto the bed, my legs falling open in response.

My heart pounds in my chest as I watch Dash lower his head between my thighs, his tongue tracing the contours of my pussy. The sensation is exquisite, and I can't help but gasp at the pleasure coursing through my body.

"God, you taste so good, Lilliana," Dash murmurs, not pausing in his ministrations as he laps up my wetness, his tongue expertly teasing my clit.

"Dash...Daddy...I need you," I moan, my fingers tangling in his jet-black hair, pulling him closer as the intensity of my pleasure builds.

"Tell me how much you want it, baby girl," Dash growls, lifting his eyes to lock onto mine, and I can see the hunger burning within them.

"Please, Daddy, don't stop. I'm so close," I whimper,

feeling the pressure inside me mounting to an almost unbearable level.

"Come for me, Lilliana," Dash commands, his voice full of authority, pushing me over the edge into a mind-shattering orgasm that leaves me breathless and quivering beneath him.

As we lie entwined in each other's arms, spent from our passionate encounter, I realize that Dash bringing me here where he can have me all alone isn't just about physical pleasure. It's about deepening our emotional connection, with Dash proving his love and commitment by being there for me in every way possible with no distractions.

His methods may be questionable, but I can't deny the way he makes me feel.

CHAPTER THIRTEEN

Lilliana

"YOU MADE ME FEEL INCREDIBLE," I whisper, my voice breathy and filled with desire. "Now it's your turn." My green eyes lock onto his piercing blue ones, a challenge and an invitation all at once.

"Are you sure, baby girl?" Dash asks, his voice low and full of desire, yet laced with concern. It's clear that this is unfamiliar territory for him, but he's willing to take the risk if it means sharing this intimate moment with me. He's usually the dominant one. He's not used to giving up control to anyone, so the fact that he's willing to let me do this is humbling and gives me a rush of power.

"Absolutely," I reply, determination surging through me. I want to make him feel just as amazing as he did for me. As I lower myself between his legs, I can't help but feel a thrill of excitement at exploring this new side of myself.

My hands grasp Dash's thighs, feeling the muscles beneath his skin tense and relax in anticipation. A small smile plays on my lips as I lean forward, inhaling his masculine scent before pressing my lips to the tip of his cock. I hear a sharp intake of breath from above me, and it only serves to fuel my desire further.

"God, Lilliana..." Dash groans as I take him into my mouth, swirling my tongue around his length. The taste of him is intoxicating, and I find myself wanting more. His strong hands tangle in my long, wavy brown hair, guiding me as I suck him deeper.

"Fuck, baby girl, you're so good at this," Dash praises, his words laced with lust and surprise. I can tell that he's struggling to maintain control, and it fills me with a sense of power. I want to make him feel like he's never felt before; I want to bring him to the edge and beyond.

As I continue sucking him off, I let my hands roam

up his chiseled abs, teasing his nipples with my fingertips. I can feel his body trembling beneath my touch, and I know that he's close. The thought of him coming in my mouth sends a shiver down my spine, igniting a fire within me that I didn't know existed.

"Fuck, Lilliana, I'm so close..." Dash pants, his hips bucking gently as I take him deeper into my throat. I can feel his cock pulsating against my tongue, and I know that he's on the verge of losing control. "Please... let me come in your mouth."

"Give it to me, Daddy," I moan around his length, the words sending a thrill through me. This newfound kink is exhilarating, and I can't wait to explore more with Dash by my side.

Dash's body tenses before he finally lets out a deep, guttural moan, his hot seed filling my mouth. I swallow every last drop, savoring the taste and the feeling of accomplishment. As I release him from my lips, I look up at Dash, my eyes filled with a mixture of satisfaction and hunger.

"Thank you, baby girl," Dash breathes, his blue eyes darkened with lust and love. "That was incredible."

I smile, my heart swelling with pride and happiness. In this moment, I know that we've reached a new level of intimacy, one that has only just begun to reveal itself. Together, we'll continue to push boundaries and explore our deepest desires. And I can't wait for what's to come.

CHAPTER FOURTEEN

Lilliana

THE CRACKLING fire casts flickering shadows across the cozy cabin, illuminating Dash's sculpted body as he lies tangled in the silk sheets beside me. His piercing blue eyes are locked on mine, filled with both vulnerability and determination. I can feel my heart beating faster in anticipation of what he's about to share.

"Listen, Lilliana..." Dash begins, his voice deep and steady. "There's something I need to tell you about my past, and how I got involved with Lucas King."

My curiosity piqued, I shift closer to him, our

naked bodies brushing against each other. His warm skin sends shivers down my spine. "Tell me, Dash. I want to know everything about you," I say, caressing his strong jawline.

"Okay," he sighs, taking a deep breath. "Years ago, I got caught up in some bad shit. Desperate for money, I ended up working for Lucas. At first, it was just small jobs, but soon enough, I found myself neck-deep in the criminal world."

As he speaks, his fingers trace slow circles on my hip, teasing me with their light touch. My desire for him grows with every word, wanting not only his body but also his trust. I watch his face, seeing the pain mixed with longing in his gaze.

"Dash," I murmur, running my hand through his jet-black hair, urging him to continue.

"Lucas isn't a man you can easily walk away from. He knows what buttons to push, how to manipulate people. But when I met you, Lilliana, everything changed." Dash's voice is thick with emotion, and I feel my chest tighten with sympathy for his struggle.

"Being with you makes me want to leave that life behind," he confesses, pulling me even closer as his lips find my neck, kissing me tenderly. "I want a fresh start, a new life with you."

"God, Dash," I whisper, feeling my body

responding to his words and his touch. The thought of him leaving that dangerous world for me ignites a fire deep within me, fueling my desire for him.

"Show me how much you want that new life, Daddy," I purr, pressing my lips to his as he groans in response. "Show me just how much you need me."

"Fuck, Lilliana," Dash growls, his eyes darkening with lust. He flips me onto my back, pinning my wrists above my head with one strong hand while the other slips between my legs, teasing me mercilessly. "You have no idea what you do to me."

"Then show me, Daddy. Show me how much you want to leave that life behind and be with me," I challenge, arching my back and biting my lip, desperate for more.

Dash's eyes flash with determination, and I know that he will prove his commitment to me in the most primal way possible. As our bodies entwine, passion and love collide, driving us both towards a future free from the darkness of his past.

CHAPTER FIFTEEN

Lilliana

THE DIM LIGHT of the room casts shadows on Dash's chiseled jawline, highlighting his piercing blue eyes that seem to see right through me. My heart races with a mix of fear and excitement as I consider the gravity of our situation. We've just decided to work together to escape the criminal world we've become entangled in, and to protect ourselves from Lucas King.

"Alright, Lilliana," Dash says, his voice a low rumble that sends shivers down my spine. "We need a plan, and we need to stick to it. No matter what."

My insides clench at the sound of his authoritative tone. Unable to resist the urge to play along, I bite my lip and reply, "Yes, Daddy."

His eyes darken with lust as he steps closer, his large hands gripping my waist firmly. "First, we need to gather intel on Lucas and his operations. Find out where his weaknesses lie."

"Good idea," I moan softly, feeling the heat pooling between my thighs as he pulls me against his hard body. "How are we going to do that?"

"By playing our roles perfectly," he murmurs, leaning down to nip at my earlobe, making me gasp. "You'll use your marketing expertise to get close to him, gather information about his businesses and allies. And I'll use my connections to find out how deep his influence goes."

I whimper, my body trembling with anticipation as one of his hands slides up my thigh, teasingly close to my aching core. "That sounds dangerous. What if he catches on to us?"

"Then we'll be ready for him," Dash growls, pressing a finger against my entrance, making me buck against him. "We'll have plans in place, escape routes, and backup. We can't let him win, Lilliana."

I pant, desperate for him to fill me up. "I'll do anything you say."

"Good girl," he praises, pushing his finger inside me and making me cry out in pleasure. "Now let's get to work, and when we're done...I'll give you the reward you deserve."

As Dash withdraws his touch and steps back, I know there's no turning back now. We're in this together against Lucas King and the criminal world that threatens to consume us both. My lust for Dash has transformed into something deeper, an unbreakable bond forged by our shared desire for freedom and each other.

"Let's do it," I whisper, my mind focused on the mission at hand, but my body still longing for the release only Dash can provide. And with that, we set off to plot our escape from the dangerous web we've found ourselves entangled in.

CHAPTER SIXTEEN

Lilliana

"DASH, WE CAN'T DO THIS," I whisper, my heart racing as his hands find their way around my waist. His grip is strong and possessive, sending shivers down my spine.

We've found out everything Dash needs to know to know what we should do next, but what he's suggesting is crazy.

"Yes, we can, Lilliana," he murmurs into my ear, his breath hot against my skin. "Let's make a new life together, away from all of this."

His words stir something deep within me, something that has been buried beneath years of cautious living and striving for perfection. He makes me feel alive in ways I never knew possible, and it's intoxicating.

"Tell me how, Dash," I breathe, needing to know that there's a way out for us.

As our bodies press closer together, the heat between us becoming impossible to ignore, Dash outlines a daring plan—one that involves faking our deaths and disappearing without a trace. It's risky, but the thought of being free to explore our desires without judgment or fear is too tantalizing to resist.

"Are you sure you're ready for this, Lilliana?" he asks, his blue eyes piercing into mine. "There's no turning back once we start."

I hesitate for a moment, weighing the consequences of what we're about to do. But then I remember the fire that burns within me every time he touches me, the way my body aches for him even when we're apart, and I know there's only one answer.

"Take me with you, Daddy," I whisper, sealing our fate. "I'll follow you anywhere."

"Good girl," Dash growls approvingly, his hand sliding up my thigh and sending a wave of pleasure through me. "Now let's get to work."

As we immerse ourselves in the intricate details of

our escape plan, our relationship becomes more intense and passionate than ever. Every stolen touch, every heated glance, only serves to strengthen the bond between us. We're a team now, united by our shared desire for freedom and each other.

"Dash," I moan as his fingers tease my most sensitive spot, "I can't wait any longer. I need you inside me."

"Patience, baby girl," he replies, his voice husky with lust. "We'll have all the time in the world once we've put this plan into action."

And so, fueled by our passion and determination, we plot our escape from the mundane lives we've been trapped in. And as I surrender myself to Dash completely, both body and soul, I know that together, we can conquer anything.

CHAPTER SEVENTEEN

Lilliana

"ARE YOU SURE ABOUT THIS?" I ask, my voice trembling with uncertainty as we prepare to execute our plan. The air is thick with tension and the scent of danger.

"Trust me, Lilliana," Dash responds, his piercing blue eyes locking onto mine, radiating confidence. "I've got this under control." He reaches out and gently brushes a strand of my long, wavy brown hair behind my ear. His touch sends shivers down my spine, making me forget momentarily about our perilous situation.

"Alright," I whisper, trying to ignore the knot in my stomach. I can't help but be drawn to Dash's magnetic presence, even though I know there's so much more to him than meets the eye. As we make our final preparations, I find my thoughts wandering to the passionate nights we've spent together, exploring each other's bodies and desires. The way he'd take control, calling me his dirty little girl while I'd beg for more, addressing him as "Daddy" — it was intoxicating.

"Ready?" Dash asks, bringing me back to reality. I nod, taking a deep breath. We're just about to put our plan into motion when the door bursts open, revealing Detective Angela Mitchell.

"Freeze!" she shouts, aiming her gun at Dash, her face set with determination. "Dash Harper, you're under arrest for your involvement in Lucas King's crimes."

"Detective Mitchell," Dash sneers, his confident facade momentarily faltering. "You're too late. You won't stop us."

"Dash, what's going on?" I stammer, feeling my heart race as the gravity of the situation sinks in. All the dirty talk, kink, and wild nights seem like a distant dream compared to the harsh reality unfolding before me.

"Sorry, Lilliana," Dash says, not taking his eyes off

the detective. "This is the part of my past I couldn't tell you about."

Detective Mitchell moves forward, handcuffing Dash with swift precision. As Dash is led away, I feel my eyes well up with tears. All the love, lust, and trust we had built over time seems to be slipping through my fingers like sand.

"Will I ever see him again?" I wonder aloud, searching Detective Mitchell's steely gaze for answers.

"Who knows," she replies coldly, her focus solely on Dash. "That's up to the justice system now."

As they leave, I'm left standing alone in our hideout, feeling hollow and devastated. The man who had awakened my deepest desires and made me feel alive was now gone, caught in the tangled web of his past.

CHAPTER EIGHTEEN

Lilliana

THE RAIN FALLS HEAVILY OUTSIDE, streaking the windowpanes and distorting my view of the city below. I'm perched on the edge of my bed, wringing my hands anxiously as my thoughts race. Dash is in jail, and there's nothing I can do about it. The weight of our love hangs heavy on my chest, almost suffocating me. My life has been anything but dull since I met him, but maybe that's what I need—to return to the predictable and safe existence I had before.

"Come on, Lilliana," Sophie says, sitting beside me and placing a comforting hand on my back. "You don't honestly believe that walking away from Dash is the best thing for you, do you?"

I try to keep my voice steady, but it trembles anyway. "I don't know, Soph. I just...My life was so much simpler before I met him. And now he's in jail, and I don't know if I can handle all this."

Sophie shakes her head, her blonde hair falling over her shoulders. "Lilliana, don't let fear control your decisions. You deserve excitement, passion, and love. Dash clearly means a lot to you, and you mean a lot to him. Sometimes you just have to take a risk and fight for what you want."

Her words resonate with me, echoing the desires that have been simmering beneath the surface of my carefully constructed exterior. Dash has awoken something within me, a craving for more than just the mundane. But my cautious nature rears its ugly head, making me question whether I should allow myself to succumb to these desires.

"Dash...he's not perfect, I know that. But he makes me feel alive, Soph. When I'm with him, I don't think about work, or deadlines, or any of the other things that usually consume me." I pause, taking a shaky breath. "He makes me feel wanted, desired...like I'm the only thing that matters."

"Then why walk away from him?" Sophie asks, her

tone gentle yet insistent. "You know you'd be giving up something special if you do."

I close my eyes for a moment, allowing Dash's touch to consume my thoughts – the way his strong hands gripped my hips as he pressed me against the wall, whispering filthy promises into my ear. The intensity of his gaze, blue eyes locked onto mine as he called me his good girl, coaxing me into embracing my submissive side.

"Because..." I admit, opening my eyes and meeting Sophie's concerned stare, "I'm scared. I'm scared of losing control, of letting go and giving in to these desires that Dash has awakened in me. And I'm terrified of what people would think if they knew about us, about our...kinks."

Sophie squeezes my hand reassuringly. "Lilliana, listen to me. You need to follow your heart. If Dash is what you want, fight for him. Don't let fear hold you back from experiencing happiness and pleasure. Life is too short to worry about what others think."

"Dash needs someone who will stand by him, no matter what." Sophie continues, conviction in her voice. "And I believe that person is you, Lilliana. You're stronger than you give yourself credit for."

Her words bolster my resolve, providing the courage I desperately needed. She's right; I can't allow fear to dictate my life. Dash may be a risk, but he's a risk worth taking. And if our love means fighting for him, then that's exactly what I'll do.

"Thank you, Sophie," I murmur, hugging her tightly. "You always know what to say."

"Hey, that's what best friends are for," she replies, a smile taking shape on her lips. "Now let's figure out how to help Dash and show the world just how strong and fearless Lilliana Thompson can be."

CHAPTER NINETEEN

Lilliana

MY HEART RACES as I push open the heavy wooden doors to the courtroom. The room is packed and filled with an air of anticipation. I scan the crowd and my eyes lock onto Dash, sitting at the defendant's table. His jet-black hair is neatly combed back, his piercing blue eyes fixed on me. For a moment, we share a connection that transcends our surroundings.

"Order in the court!" the bailiff shouts, and I take a deep breath, gathering my courage. This is it. This is the moment when I'll finally admit my love for Dash, despite the risks and consequences.

"Your Honor," I - I

"Your Honor," I begin, my voice wavering slightly. "I have a statement to make."

The judge, an older man with a stern expression, eyes me warily before nodding his approval. "Very well, Miss Thompson. Proceed."

My pulse quickens as I step forward, feeling the weight of every gaze in the room. Dash remains stoic, but I can sense the curiosity and unease beneath his confident exterior.

"Your Honor, members of the jury, I stand before you today not as a witness, but as someone who loves Dash Harper deeply and unconditionally." The words flow from my heart, my green eyes never leaving Dash's face. "Our love story may have started under unconventional circumstances, but our connection is real and undeniable."

Whispers fill the room, yet my focus remains on Dash, whose eyes reveal a mixture of surprise and vulnerability. It's now or never. I need to convince the judge that Dash deserves another chance.

"Dash has made mistakes in his life, as we all have. But even with his dark past, he has shown kindness, generosity, and courage. He risked his own safety to protect me from Lucas King, the very man whose organization he was once a part of." My voice grows stronger, more determined. "Dash isn't the same person he was back then, and I believe he genuinely wants to right his wrongs."

The judge leans back in his chair, clearly contemplating my words. "Miss Thompson, are you suggesting that Mr. Harper should be given the opportunity to cooperate with law enforcement in bringing down Mr. King's criminal organization?"

"Yes, Your Honor," I reply without hesitation. "If anyone can provide valuable information and insights into Lucas King's operation, it's Dash. And if there's one thing I know about him, it's that he wouldn't squander this chance at redemption."

"Very well," the judge says, stroking his chin thoughtfully. "Mr. Harper, would you be willing to cooperate with law enforcement in exchange for a reduced sentence?"

Dash looks straight at me, his blue eyes intense and full of gratitude. Slowly, he nods. "Yes, Your Honor."

"Then let it be so," the judge declares. "The court will take Miss Thompson's testimony into consideration. Mr. Harper's sentence shall be reduced under the condition that he fully cooperates with law enforcement in bringing down Lucas King's organization."

Relief washes over me, but I know our journey is far from over. As the courtroom erupts in murmurs, I lock eyes with Dash once more, silently vowing to stand by him every step of the way.

CHAPTER TWENTY

Dash

THE COLD METAL of the prison gate gives way to the taste of sweet freedom as it creaks open, revealing Lilliana in the hazy afternoon light. Her long, wavy brown hair frames her vibrant green eyes that are full of hope and desire. She's waiting for me, and the sight of her makes my heart race.

"Dash," she breathes out, her voice wavering with emotion. I can't help but smirk, knowing how much she's missed me. I've missed her too, more than words can express.

"Lilliana," I say, closing the distance between us

with a few long strides. "You have no idea how much I've dreamed of this moment."

"Show me," she teases, her lip caught between her teeth, daring me to take control. As a risk-taker, I'm no stranger to pushing the boundaries, and I know she craves excitement and passion.

"Only if you promise to be a good girl for Daddy," I reply, my voice low and seductive.

"Always," she purrs, leaning in for a scorching kiss. Our mouths collide in a dance of lust and longing, tongues intertwining and exploring every inch of each other. My hands grip her waist, pulling her closer to feel the heat of her body against mine.

"Did you miss me, baby girl?" I growl into her ear, nibbling on her lobe.

"God, yes," she moans, gripping onto my biceps. "I've been so lost without you."

"Let me make it up to you," I say, my mind racing with thousands of ways to prove my love and commitment. But there's one grand gesture I know will leave her speechless. "Lilliana Thompson, will you marry me?"

Her eyes widen in shock, the surprise evident on her beautiful face. In her moments of vulnerability, I see the perfectionist within her, always striving for more in life. She's my perfect match.

"Dash... Are you serious?" she stammers, barely able to contain her excitement.

"Never been more serious in my life," I reply, kneeling down and holding her hand. "I want to spend the rest of my life showing you how much I love you, how much I'm willing to fight for us."

"Then yes, a thousand times yes," she exclaims, tears welling up in her eyes as she pulls me back up into a passionate kiss.

"Good," I whisper, smirking against her lips. "Now let's celebrate by getting you naked and reminding you who you belong to."

"Only if we can be filthy together," she whispers, her gaze full of pure lust.

"Deal," I promise, guiding her towards the car parked nearby. Our journey of love and commitment is just beginning, but I know we'll conquer every obstacle thrown our way. Together, we're unstoppable.

CHAPTER TWENTY-ONE

Lilliana

THE SUN SETS over our quaint new home, painting the sky with warm hues of orange and pink. Dash wraps his strong arms around me as we stand on the porch, admiring the peaceful scene before us. It's hard to believe that we've managed to escape Lucas King's grip and start anew.

"Can you believe it, Lilliana? We're finally free," Dash whispers in my ear, his breath sending shivers down my spine.

I lean back into his embrace, feeling his warmth

and strength. "Free and together," I reply, a smile tugging at the corner of my lips.

Dash's hand slides down to rest on my hip, his fingers gently squeezing in a possessive manner. I can't help but feel a surge of excitement at the prospect of exploring this newfound freedom with him.

"Let's go inside," he suggests, his voice thick with desire. "I want to show you just how much I've missed you."

As we enter the cozy living room, Dash wastes no time in pulling me close, his lips crashing against mine in a passionate, heated kiss. My heart races with anticipation as I wrap my arms around his neck, eager to lose myself in his touch.

"Dash, I need you," I gasp, breaking away from the kiss. "I need you to take control, to make me yours completely."

His eyes darken with lust, and he grins wickedly. "You want me to be your daddy, baby girl?"

"More than anything," I breathe, feeling my cheeks flush at the admission.

Dash leads me upstairs to our bedroom, his hand gripping mine firmly. Once inside, he shuts the door and locks it, trapping us in our own private world of pleasure.

"Strip for me, Lilliana," he commands, sitting on the edge of the bed and watching me intently.

I oblige, shedding my clothes slowly, baring myself to him completely. Dash's gaze never wavers, his eyes drinking in every inch of my exposed skin.

"Good girl," he praises, his voice low and husky. "Come here."

I obey, standing before him as he remains seated on the bed. His hands roam over my body, caressing and teasing my most sensitive spots. I squirm under his touch, desperate for more.

"Please, Daddy," I whimper, my need for him overwhelming me.

"Patience, baby girl," Dash murmurs, his fingers dipping between my thighs. "I'm going to take my time with you tonight."

As Dash explores my body, his confidence and dominance make me feel safe, cherished, and desired like never before. This new life, free from the shadows of our past, holds so much promise and passion for us both. Together, we will embrace it fully, surrendering ourselves to each other without fear or hesitation.

CHAPTER TWENTY-TWO

Dash

SUNLIGHT STREAMS through the windows as I watch Lilliana, her wavy brown hair cascading down her back as she meticulously arranges items on the shelves. The warm glow highlights her bright green eyes, making them sparkle like emeralds. We've finally opened our small business together, combining her marketing expertise with my artistic vision.

"Dash, what do you think of this setup?" she asks, stepping back to survey her work.

I walk over and wrap my arms around her waist, pulling her close. "It looks perfect, just like everything else you do," I whisper into her ear, feeling her body shudder slightly at the sound of my voice.

"Thank you, Daddy," she replies, emphasizing the last word in a sultry tone that sends a thrill down my spine. Our shared passion for each other has unlocked new desires and fantasies we never thought possible.

"Let's take a break," I suggest, my hands roaming her body, igniting a familiar heat between us.

"Here?" she questions playfully, her excitement evident in her voice.

"Here," I confirm, my lips finding hers in a passionate kiss as I press her against the newly stocked shelves. She moans softly into my mouth, her hands gripping my shoulders, urging me on.

"Tell me what you want, baby girl," I demand, my voice low and commanding.

"Please, Daddy," she begs, her voice breathless and needy, "fuck me right here, right now."

"Naughty girl," I murmur, my fingers making quick work of her clothing, the urgency of our desire taking over. As I strip her down, exposing her beautiful, naked body, her cheeks flush with a mixture of arousal and embarrassment.

"Anyone could walk in," she whispers, her eyes flicking to the door.

"Then let them see how much I adore you," I

growl, lifting her onto the counter. I waste no time in claiming her, our bodies moving together with a well-practiced rhythm.

"God, Daddy, you feel so good," she moans, her nails digging into my back as we lose ourselves in each other.

"Mine," I grunt possessively, feeling her tighten around me as we reach our climax together.

As we catch our breath, our sweaty skin pressed against each other, I press a gentle kiss to her forehead. "I love you, Lilliana."

"I love you too, Dash."

Our love continues to grow and thrive in this new life we've built together. Our small business is more than just a shared dream. It's a testament to our passion, our commitment, and our trust in one another. And although the darkness of my past still lingers, I find solace in the love and light that Lilliana brings to my life.

EPILOGUE

Lilliana

AS I STAND at the altar, my heart races in anticipation. The scent of fresh roses wafts through the air, and the sound of gentle violin music fills the room. To my left, Dash's eyes pierce into me with their vibrant blue hue, igniting a fire within my soul that burns with desire.

"Dash," I begin, my voice shaking slightly as I recite our vows. "From the moment we met, your confidence and passion swept me off my feet. You've shown me a world I never knew existed and pushed me to explore desires I never thought possible."

Dash's lips tilt into a crooked grin, his eyes flaring with heat as his strong hands gripping mine. "Lilliana, you're my perfect little angel," he says, his tone dripping with lust. "I promise to be your rock, your protector, and your lover. Together, we'll conquer anything life throws at us."

As our friends and family watch, tears glisten in their eyes, moved by the intensity of our love. My mind drifts back to the nights we spent tangled in each other's arms, exploring every inch of one another's bodies, lost in the throes of ecstasy. The way Dash would whisper in my ear, calling me his dirty little girl, his good girl, only served to heighten my arousal.

I whisper so only he can hear, my private vow to him, "Dash, I vow to support you as we face life's challenges together. I promise to be your safe haven, your confidant, and your partner in crime. And, most importantly, I will always be your naughty little girl, ready to please you however you desire."

"Good girl," Dash whispers, his voice low and sultry, sending shivers down my spine. He leans in, capturing my lips in a searing kiss filled with promises of passion and devotion. Our connection is electric, leaving no doubt in my mind that we are meant to be together.

"By the power vested in me," the officiant declares,

"I now pronounce you husband and wife. You may kiss the bride."

Dash wraps his arms around me, pulling me close and pressing his lips against mine. Our tongues dance together, a tantalizing preview of the passion to come. I can feel his bulging hardness pressed against my thigh, reminding me that he is always ready for action.

As we break our kiss, I gaze into Dash's eyes, smiling at the thought of our future together. We will face whatever comes our way, knowing that our love will conquer all obstacles.

"Are you ready for the honeymoon, daddy?" I whisper seductively in his ear.

"Always," he responds, grinning wickedly as his hand caresses my lower back, his eyes full of promises of the pleasures to come.

9 798223 075523